CASE BY CASE BASIS

Also by Patricia Willers

Wandering Canalside

CASE BY CASE BASIS

There are at least two sides to every story.

stories by Patricia Willers

sketches by Natalie Willers

ISBN: 0-9898842-2-8

ISBN-13: 978-0-9898842-2-8

The following is a work of fiction. All characters are fictional, and all places and incidents are used fictitiously. Any resemblance to real people is coincidental.

patriciawillers.com

Library of Congress Control Number: 2016903387
Patricia Willers, Davis, California

10 9 8 7 6 5 4 3 2 1

For Gordon, Sophie, Allen, & Lillian

Contents

The Acknowledgements Story

Welcome to a book of short stories.

I don't write short stories, I was quite sure of that fact. That is, until a few years ago, when I joined a couple of friends at a local Irish pub to talk writing. One guy had a book of short travel stories in the works, another had a blog of random, half or fully true stories. We met, we chatted, and a few things happened all at once and quite quickly. First, I combed through every computer and USB I had and compiled a complete and collected folder of my writing. Yes, my organizational system is about as helpful and sensical as ewoks flying through a forest on speeder bikes. No planning and not very productive, but the process *is* quite fun to watch.

I soon realized that the loads of "snippets of future novels" that I had were oftentimes already short stories. How had I never noticed?

The Acknowledgements Story

We, the members of my writing group, then decided we should produce something new each week, so I tried, and it was fun. I began reading short stories and writing more and more of them. They were just so satisfying! Read one in a few hours, sometimes a few minutes, done! Write a first draft, send it on to a friend and get feedback by the end of the night! What a fabulous new world to explore.

In no time at all, I had a book (a document) jammed with stories—20 or 30—too many, yes, but wow! I had written, started, and even finished so many over the years. They came out eclectic, a mishmash of all the lives you could have or may have lived. That's the truth; please keep that in mind.

There's a reason this section was placed at the beginning of the book this time. I always wondered why people did that. Why not at the end? Now I understand, however. There are things that I need to say, elements I need to make known, before people dive in to this particular collection of tales.

For all the members of my family, I hope you kept reading to this point. I have been putting this off, delaying it to the last possible moment. Some, many, or all of these stories will shock you.

I am not old, yet I feel I have already lived one hell of a life. It's been great, don't worry! However, that doesn't mean that I haven't been around the world, broke, had a great job, had a great boss and had a horrible boss. I've made good decisions and bad decisions and sometimes no decisions at all. I've laughed so hard I cried and cried so hard I laughed, and drunk too much and drunk too little, considering the situation. Just life. Nothing special or unordinary about it, right?

All of those experiences, and more, have gone into the heart and soul and densely Minnesotan backbone of this book. It's fictional. I beg of you to remember that.

For a while, I had it in my head to wait until after my grandparents had passed away to publish these stories. I was worried it would be taken the wrong way, that I would be misunderstood. But why!? $#$%!? would I do that? My grandparents are the best. I have four, (yes, four) of the strongest and spunkiest 80-year-olds on Earth in my family tree. My grandma Sophie was the first child in her family to be born in North America. She's been keeping Slovak treats (kolache) alive and baking for 82 years. My grandpa Gordon, who gave me the Danish genes that make me who I am, has his own company. He taught me about perseverance and puns (N-Rich!) He's also really good at card games. Watch it, he might not be following suit...

My grandma Lil ran a diner in San Diego in the early fifties. My Grandpa Al (that's Grandpa Al™ at Luverne Elementary School) was in the military for almost 30 years. When he went off to war, my grandmother stayed in San Diego and made

Minnesotan pies for SoCal construction workers. What!?! So brave. So very, very brave. She also stayed up late watching "The Sound of Music" with me when I was a little girl.

As I said, my Grandpa Allen is a somewhat renowned figure at the local elementary school. He learned how to play "Go Fish" in his 80s. Before that he was simply busy working. He's still working, in fact. As far as I can tell, he's had his hip and both shoulders replaced just so he can keep up with the 40-year-olds in average hours worked per week. He always wins.

With all this, and so, so much more, what more could I ask for!?

Thanks, G&G and G&G. I love you and all the rest in my family that came before and after.

I need to thank a fair number of people for help on this one. Yes, it all started when I restarted attending weekly writing clubs, so thank you to Ryan Hedrick, an ever supportive, albeit a little pornographic, voice and writing buddy. Next is Mike Lemcke ("On a Bender Abroad," now available), who is a gem of a guy. Thanks, guys. Writing and talking writing with y'all was always fun. Berryessa Brewing Company also played a role. Thank you for Markley Cove. I had so many of those during Writin' Club.

Thanks also to Joseph Hill for his insight and wisdom into the world of creative writing. The first time I met up with Joseph, part of writer's club #2, he quoted Kafka and Walden. I think. I was super intimidated, and I felt like a child who'd never written anything in my life. I needed that just like I needed him to say, "I see what you're trying to do, but I don't think you did it." That was a very nice way of saying: REDO! And I needed it and appreciated it. Thanks!

Veronica, thank you for both the pozole (yum!!) and the title of your pozole eating Facebook group, "Pozole, because rain."

Thanks to Alyssa Glawe and Auger Goma for their input on French linguistics. And a huge thanks to Jane Riese for her careful eye and extremely helpful insight on these stories. Still to thank are Teresa Pargeter, Sandy Bosch, Melissa Oeding and Christina, for discussion, pre-reads and re-reads, and answering my many sporadic questions regarding which or what is better or worse or cut or kept.

My youngest sister Natalie is my illustrator. It's her talent and creativity that provide the sketches in charcoal and black ink. Natalie has been amazing throughout the writing and editing process, always available with feedback and new ideas, or just for a laugh when I needed it.

Her drawings started as a simple idea. One after another she drew them, for fun or for a creative release amongst studying and reading—while working towards her nursing degree! I came to see that this situation was not only working, it was amazing. I loved the pictures and how they related to my stories, and soon I had one for each. Thank you so much, Natalie, for embarking on this journey of a project with me over the last few years. You have made it all the more enjoyable! And keep drawing. You have a knack that's worthy of a spotlight. Lumos!

Oh, & Matt.

The rest is really history. Whether funny, scary, horrifying, happy, sad, cheerful, deep, shallow, confident, dramatic, intensely awkward, outdoor, indoor, wonderful, curious, odd, utterly ridiculous, feminine, masculine, worthwhile, worthless, dominant, dependent, valuable, valued, heartfelt, joyous, gay, young, old, confused, confusing…

There's just a little bit of truth in everything, it's always more complicated than you think, and there are at least two sides to every story. Some, alas, are fucked up.

Listen, consider, contemplate, and decide—on a Case by Case Basis.

Street Food for Days

"Hey."

"Hey," she paused. "You made it."

"Ya. Have you already ordered?"

"Nope, waiting for you."

"Not too long?"

"No," she replied, leaving an indicative pause. "So how've you been? How was your day?"

"Good. I've been busy, but only because Randy and I went away last weekend to camp at some hot springs. So I got all backed up."

"That's too bad."

"Nah, it's fine. It was totally worth it, soaking away my worries."

"Aww, nice. How's it going with Randy, by the way?"

"Yeah, good. It has been better lately."

"Yeah? Great."

"He's doing that penile thing, you know? And that's helped."

They both paused for a moment.

"Penile? I don't think I heard about this. What does that mean, exactly?"

"Oh," she allowed an extended pause. "well, he had been- had been feeling kind of depressed about the whole job thing, and his libido was near nothing. So he asked around—discretely, obvs—and did some research and now he's on this herbal remedy for uh-enhancement, plus whey smoothies or some nonsense."

"O-k."

"I looked it up and read about it; I'm sure it doesn't actually do anything, but he's doing something about the problem—that works for me. It's been a great month in bed."

"Well, great. I didn't even know there had been issues, but I'm glad there aren't anymore."

"Yeah, me too." The pause was pregnant. "How's work for you?"

"Oh, not bad. I'm just going along—it doesn't change a whole lot day to day, to be honest."

"But you like it, right?"

"Yes," she replied after a brief, but honest pause, "I do. It's interesting and stable. And I get long lunches. That's nice."

"Sure."

"Not a lot of vacation, unfortunately."

"That's too bad."

"Yeah." She paused, open mouthed. "But I don't really go anywhere anyway, I suppose."

"How do you use the time that you have?"

"I don't."

"Oh, that reminds me." She paused as a smile broke slyly across her face. "At the hot springs, thanks to this whole 'enhancement project,' Randy was just walking around the whole time with a boner. Cracks me up."

"Wait, was it a nude hot springs?"

"Yeah, of course. Swimsuits are for sissies." She paused and barked a laugh. "At least he was ready to pound me at a moment's notice."

"Whoa, holy shit."

"What?" She paused, wondering what was wrong with what she'd said. "What'd I say?"

"Never mind. Ugh, finally. Our turn."

"Finally."

"What do you want?"

"I'll have the pulled pork sandwich with mac 'n' cheese. Slaw on the side."

"The same for me. Yum. I love food trucks."

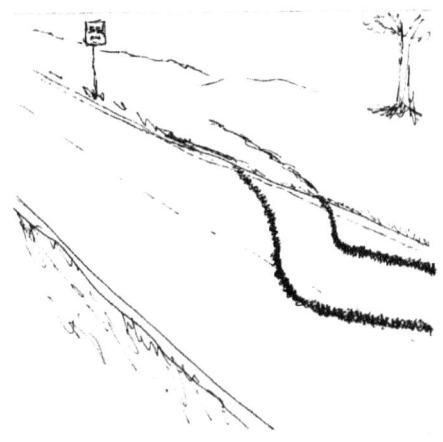

He Has Multiple Personalities

The first time I met my husband's family was kind of an ordeal. He's chill; his parents are great; his sister is sweet. I met them early on and it was all very good.

His older brother, interestingly enough, has multiple personality disorder. I was introduced to this idea very, very slowly. It's difficult to become part of a family, and I guess for some people, this piece of information could be the straw that breaks the camel's back. In my case, it was not, but that doesn't mean that Tucker wasn't worried about us both.

As we dated early on and got to know each other, Tucker talked about his family often. I noticed that there was always a bit of awkwardness when his brother Jonathon came up. I'm sure that Tucker thought he was avoiding it effectively, but it was very clear to me from the start that he loved him and that they got along well—but also that there was a secret surrounding his health; I had no idea what.

The big meeting day was all planned for the Fourth of July. Outside in his parents' backyard there would be barbequing and friends, some cousins, and time around the pool. As mentioned, I'd actually already met his sister individually. She lived near us in the city, and his parents had met us for dinner once or twice as well. I hadn't met the cousins or any of the family friends.

On this particular grilling holiday, a grand barbeque, I believe the hope was that by surrounding Jonathon with all the people that he knew well and was comfortable with, his personality would be at least minimally collected. Personally, I wasn't sure how this type of disorder functioned—or transpired at all, really. I could tell that Tucker was nervous, though. He wanted the best for his brother, yes; and he also wanted me to feel comfortable with his family.

It sounds weird, I know, but I suppose if someone has multiple personality disorder, then it's like they are many different people. There's going to be one that you prefer over the others.

The one they all liked was something like a 14-year-old country schoolboy. He was boyish, carefree, sweet, and totally addicted to scale modeling. My theory was that this caused him to have a lot of focus, so they felt like he was occupied. They worried about him less. As one would probably assume, Jonathon still lived under the care of his parents.

On the much anticipated day, Tucker drove down with his sister to help his parents get everything set up, so I left late morning to make my way there. About halfway, out of the blue, something small and furry ran in front of my car. I swerved out of the way no problem, but for one terrifying moment I caught the abrupt edge of the shoulder. Being unable to pull the car back onto the road was a horrible feeling, but luckily, it evened out a little and I had the sense and ability to keep control, slow down, and pull over. Only one large oleander paid the price of the pull-off.

I was never that good of a driver. I just don't do it often enough. Why drive when the bus stop was 50 feet from my house? A/C, heat—it had it all—and with an unlimited monthly pass for the price of half a tank of gas? But I digress.

On the side of the road I took a minute for me. No harm done really. Even the little rascal lived, but I was still shaken up. I called Tucker to see how things were going there. Fortunately for me and unfortunately for all, I received word that they were having troubles at the house too. Jonathon was missing, never a good sign.

It hadn't been a good day, one of the worst for Jonathon in a long while. I was told that the night before and earlier that morning he had been living the role of the adrift investment banker. He was sure he had a job, and wanted desperately to get back to it. Obviously, he had nowhere real to go. He'd spent the morning storming around the house in a rage. I guess when it got really bad—this morning included—he threw things and, God forbid, drank. Never a good move in combination with instability and a true lack of sanity. The poor fellow.

It was strange. On the phone, right there in the car, just off the shoulder, with Jonathon missing and what I would soon realize was a flat tire, Tucker told me everything.

When Jonathon was a little boy, the family termed him "moody." He had the ups and downs and stubbornness and gleefulness of the terrible twos; it just lasted well into elementary school. In middle school, when they took recess and daily gym class and exercise away, it got worse. It was clear to all of them and anyone who interacted with him that he was not normal. The word *bipolar* was thrown around a lot, but those closest to him knew it wasn't the right diagnosis. It wasn't a swing back and forth. Often Jonathon didn't know who he was. Eventually, the family came to recognize that no one knew who he was. They shared stories one day, when Jonathon was spending the day with the school counselor— finally having the screening done that should have happened years before. As they shared, they saw that no one knew the same Jonathon.

To his mother, Jonathon was absentminded and a little, well, slow. He could complete menial tasks and in fact helped her out quite successfully around the house, but she had always assumed that this was about the maximum capability of her son's brain. It sounded harsh, but this is all she knew of him. His father most often got the 14-year-old version. Tucker and his sister Cecile had experienced this Jonathon on a few occasions as well, but not frequently. Cecile more often than not got a confused or angry Jonathon. Maybe because she was a female, or maybe because she was older than him, they didn't have a solid connection of any kind.

Tucker had another sort of relationship with Jonathon. They were close in age and had therefore spent a large portion of their childhood together. From what I heard from Tuck, because of this, they had kind of, sort of grown and changed together. They likely had the strongest connection, and according to Tucker, Jonathon tried the hardest to maintain "normal" with him.

In the presence of Tucker, Jonathon was a jock.

He played sports. Some days one sport in particular, sometimes all or any. Jonathon was skilled enough that he could play pretty much any sport, and contrary to their mother's read on the situation, he was quick about many things. He could easily compete, and he could be a team player, especially with Tucker. On good days, he could even be the hero. They all loved these days, when Jonathon could join a school team or even a pickup game and come home happy and feeling successful.

Why did this happen? What was it about each person that brought out a different Jonathon?

In a way, it explained why he was so strange when any number or combination of them came together. He was all confused, all mixed up.

"Hey there, can I help you out with that tire?" I jumped when a man appeared suddenly at my window, but thank goodness he was there. As much as I was relishing and appreciating this talk, I needed to be there much more than I needed to be sitting in a car on the side of the road on the phone. I apologized to Tucker and turned to the man at the window.

"Tire?"

"You have a flat tire. I assume that's why you're sitting here on the side of the road?"

He phrased it half like a question and half like a statement.

"Need a hand?"

She had driven herself right into a flat tire on the side of the road. *Damn*, her worry for small, fuzzy animals.

"Please." I asked sweetly, only with a slightly flirtatious edge. Sure, I had a boyfriend I loved and was committed to, but I also needed to get this tire changed. I got out of the car and stood next to him by the left rear wheel.

"It's flat. Hm."

"Yup, it is," he lightly replied with a small grin.

"I swerved. There was a little animal in the road. I think I messed up by going off the edge onto the shoulder."

"Swerved? I think your mistake was before the shoulder. How big was this animal?"

"Not big, maybe a rabbit or a raccoon?"

"That's… a pretty big difference. And raccoons are nocturnal. Was it a cat?"

"Oh, no! A cat!? I hope not."

"You didn't hit it."

"Oh, yeah. Of course. Phew."

I couldn't help but blush. He laughed silently and shook his head.

"With all due respect, miss, you really shouldn't swerve unless there is something large in the road, like a deer or a moose. Your car can easily handle a collision with a rabbit, or even a cat—no matter how much you like them-" He winked. "It'd be much, much worse for you to swerve and then roll your car. You could be killed."

"Oh… Thanks for the information. I didn't know."

"Well, never mind. Let's get this tire fixed and get you on the road."

His generosity was charming. When I described him to Tucker a few hours later that is exactly how I did so. He was like a southern gentleman. He knew exactly what to do, made me feel safe, and didn't creep me out or come on to me in the slightest.

"Where are you from?" I asked him once the heavy straining of the bolt removal was done. *Are they called bolts? Lugs?* His so very easygoing demeanor made me wonder what he did for a living.

"I don't actually have a job, per se. I care for my elderly mother. She's reached the point that I don't feel comfortable having her home alone."

"So you decided to do the job?"

"It's not much of a job. She's a wonderful woman."

"I know, I'm sorry. I didn't mean that."

"I didn't feel right having her live alone, and I very well couldn't tell one of my siblings to leave their careers and move back home, so I did it."

"That's very benevolent of you."

"Thank you. Could you hand me the tire iron again?"

"Of course."

"What is it that you do?"

"Me? I'm a teacher." This made him smile at me. I'm not sure why.

"High school English?"

I smiled at that. "Yes, in fact. But how could you possibly guess that? Do I have the look of a high school English teacher?"

"Hmm… That's a good question. Perhaps I have a knack with teachers."

That moment was the first that I realized that he had no vehicle. This young man was nearly as intriguing as it gets. I considered inviting him over to Tucker's when we were through, but eventually I decided that it would be too strange.

After 35 minutes, the spare was on. I asked him genuinely if he needed a ride somewhere, but he immediately declined. We were out in the middle of nowhere, so he must have had a bike or truck parked somewhere in the surrounding trees. Clearly he was competent enough to know how to get back home.

In the rearview mirror I saw him wave as I drove away down the road. Finally at Tucker's, I let myself into the yard and found the whole family congregated next to the house in lawn chairs. The look on Tuck's face told me that Jonathon was still MIA, however, they all seemed relatively calm. Tucker's mother poured me some lemonade, lightly spritzed with champagne, and sat down to wait and, for the time being, politely discuss my tire ordeal. I wanted to minimize it, seeing that they all had something much more worrisome on their minds.

"Hi everyone! Sorry I'm late." Practically the moment I finished my tale, my tire mechanic walked in through the gate. Of course. Who else would this frank and competent mystery mechanic be if not one of Tucker's cousins. I kicked myself for not having introduced myself.

"Jonathon!"

He smiled broadly at me as his family stood to hug him. I was in awe.

"I was on my way home when I came across a weary traveler. What could I do but help dear Lindy with her flat tire?" I just stared.

We formally introduced ourselves with a hug, but it was obvious now that Jonathon had known who I was the whole time.

"Why didn't you tell me?" I asked him in a hushed aside.

"Tell you what?" He winked and put his hand on Tucker's shoulder and gave it a squeeze.

It was a perfect summer evening, complete with fireworks, good barbequed meat and more champagne lemonade for everyone. At the end of the night I found myself sitting on a lawn chair with Tucker. Everyone else had gone to bed.

"Your family is wonderful, Tuckster." He smiled at me and reached his hand across to take mine.

"Everyone loved you, Lindy. And I mean everyone."

"Well, I'm glad." I was very glad. I liked them a lot too.

"Lindy."

"Yes."

"Lindy, we've never seen this one." He shook his head in disbelief. "I've never met this Jonathon." Now a smile began to show; he looked almost proud. "And he's so nice. You brought out the nicest Jonathon I've met so far. He's almost more than we could have imagined for him." Tucker reached his arms out and hugged me tightly. "Lindy, I was honest to God going to ask you to marry me this weekend. And now I know it's all right, completely and totally right. I know it. But I don't want you to think this is because of Jonathon… because somehow in one afternoon, you have created-"

"I haven't created anything."

"You have drawn out, lured out, the best version of our multiple Jonathons."

"I had nothing to do with it."

"I know, but thank you all the same, love."

L'actrice

When he came out of the dressing room, I knew exactly what to do. My role would change and I would become new. Glorified. It required confidence, balls, of which I had none, *et beaucoup pompe, beaucoup panache.*

I began to drink martinis with an olive, one green, and a tiny triangle of fresh pineapple. Yes, it seemed just the thing to do. Mary Joanne, my old self, would drink white wine, or champagne, on occasion. However, Mary Joanne was married to a notable lead actor, and had a wifely reputation to uphold. This was all gone now. A complete substitution would have to be made. There was no more Mary Joanne, and I could not, would not bear to be pitied. Rather, I would be envied. I would be glorified as *Marion*—be sure to pronounce it with a proper French accent.

It was perfect for me! I could play any lead role, only this time, I would play it for life. 'Twas no problem at all, though *biensûr*, it would have to be done gradually. A sudden personality change, well, *mes amis,* that would be crazy. But a slow reach, creeping delightfully to the tragically uncontrived matriarchal yet desirable being that I could have always been—the truth is—it had been coming all along.

I began to speak more and more French, *difficile*, it was, as I had only played a few spare roles over *les années*. It was very nearly clear to most that I was not French. However, the intrigue of another tongue and a romance-tinged name was all that I needed from the old country.

Mary Joanne was helpful and devout to all around her. She needed not to be center stage, but *Marion, oui*, I said *oui!* She was the one and only. Ideal French women of a certain age never would ever share a stage. Sister, sister, now devout to none. Understudies, good riddance and *adieu*.

Asked, one day, to play opposite him, *mais non, ce n'est pas possible!* To be asked to play a lead, *un amant* of that man! *Non!* How could I? After what he had done. A man gone gay. I would not could not look him in the eye. Not after *vingt années*. Not after spending so many years as his wife.

That awful man, he could not, would not hurt *Marion*. My dignity was at stake! And *Marion* was fully enviable. She applied powder and rouge each day alone, with her crystal Martini glass in one hand, behind a door with only one name. A star.

And then, against all my *grandes* protests, my protests *grandes*, I was forced to do so—reciting lines of love and lines *de luxure. C'est terrible!*

That man, that terrible, terribly handsome man.

Cet homme, que terrible, que beau… que homosexuel. I shan't look him in the eye. *Non, Marion* could not would not look a past lover scorned in the eye. Mary Joanne would have wept at the sight, would have wept before and after. She would have stepped aside and let Guy pass, just as the horror passed to her.

But Marion, zut alors! She may just be the type of woman who wants to kill her ex-husband over petty deeds, or simply, perhaps, for center stage.

Let me change

I was not changed
by him or her or them.
It happened and happens
with life and time.
You have too.
Have you not noticed?
So let me be changed.

Modern Tintype

Her name was Glorieta, even though nobody called her that.

She took selfies every day. Not one, but 7. Approximately every 2 hours starting at 8 a.m. when she got up to go to school. That's not even too many.

The first was in her pajamas. Selfie.

This was always the first effort at who she would be for the day. What a great world she lived in, to wake up and decide who and how you were going to be each and every day.

50 percent of the time she even chose right, first time.

A perk, Savannah thought, of the modern world. It was unfortunate that her first take be an epic fail— but necessary. These things happen. She was too sleepy at 8 a.m. to choose correctly the first time. Raquelle plus iPhone minus her medium skin mint condition mocha with white chocolate and whipped cream equaled a big fat question mark. At least half of the time.

For exactly this reason she had adjusted from 4 selfies a day to 7.

Banana for breakfast. Selfie. Camilla loved to start the day with a healthy breakfast.

By 9 a.m. she had most often settled it. At this point in the day, her friends would be visiting her SNS feeds. Likes and favorites and hearts all before first period. She adored this. Her system was not foolproof, but she was committed.

The third shot took place at noon.

Typically, no alterations occurred. Buuuut, Sammie-Sam had a great smile, and the lighting in the computer lab made her lips look just the right shade of pink.

Today she'd had an altercation with her geometry teacher. Ugh. She'd forgotten to do her homework, and Esther always did her homework, so she became Salina quickly and surely. Selfie.

She parted her hair on the other side.

At 2:23 each day, she would confirm her counseling appointment. She checked in and gave her name. For the past two appointments, she'd been Esther Randall. A lovely name for a lovely, young Jewish woman who lived on the Upper East Side. She wasn't allowed to change her address. Now she was Salina Goes for good. Oh, geometry ruins everything. Selfie.

The receptionist in the waiting room had been particularly delighted about Esther Randall. She, Sarah Receptionist, was the type of person who liked to greet everyone by name. Salina got the feeling that it bothered her that she could not greet with an appropriate level of confidence. These feelings of unease were unnecessary. Salina wondered why Dr. Wonder didn't hire a receptionist who could adequately roll with the punches. It's not like she was crazy. She simply changed her name now and again. If it bothered her that much, Sarah Receptionist could look online like the rest of the world and find out exactly who would be coming in to see the good doctor today.

Dr. Caroline Wonder, the psychologist she'd been seeing for the past two weeks, did not, in truth, wonder. The wonder was closer in meaning to wonderful. Dr. Wonder was very wonderful, in fact. As far as Salina knew, Dr. Wonder never looked up her name ahead of time. She merely waited until she entered the room, appraised her mood and appearance modestly, and invited her to join her in the sitting area nearest the windows. Glorieta loved the windows. Raquelle loved the windows. Salina loved the windows. Esther loved the windows. As far as she knew, she would always love looking out from the fourth floor onto Lilac Park. It was tragically romantic in a way she had not found her life to be.

Her mother's life was tragically romantic. Her mother, Gloria, had the same identity quirk as Glorieta, except with appearance and husbands. Attire so drastically different that it could hardly be placed in the same country, let alone the same decade, cycled in and out of her mother's closet like a spinning rolodex, a revolving door, a Twitter feed.

She was sure some famed psychologist would tell her that her issues were all caused by father issues. He'd left them both, big and little Gloria, when she was too young to remember.

Due to the fact that she knew this, and that it was so obvious, she knew it couldn't be the real reason.

Her mother remembered, so she had every right to be crazy.

On a weekly basis, when she walked into that office, at 2:25 p.m. to be precise, darling Dr. Wonder gave in to all of Bianca's impulses. Dr. Wonder always seemed to have a plan. She, personally, was less optimistic, as was her mother. But she certainly enjoyed being able to come and go through her names and selfie styles as she pleased. On breakthrough days, she would need to change everything all right away. 3:26 Selfie.

Last week she had been Gertruud. Two u's, like the Dutch like to do. That was when Dr. Wonder appeared in her life. Dr. Wonder would remain for a few more weeks; Kelsey was quite sure. The gyratory names and personalities in her life always overlapped. This helped her keep her grasp on who they all were, and perhaps who she was. Not that there was anything wrong with schizophrenia. She'd learned that from Dr. Harald Butner. Dr. Butner was a transgender psychologist. She'd liked him.

She'd been lost altogether before Dr. Butner. It's too bad he'd had to go.

Dr. Krispo came next. She was awful. She'd accused Ilena of breaking all the rules of society.

Who made these supposed rules? She wanted to know. Krispo said that in the past people had to follow societal standards, and the way that *Glorieta*—she'd refused to call her anything else—changed her name and created a fake background everyday for the "Non-existent world of the In-ter-*net*" was both alien and tasteless and would never allow her to integrate and be a part of the current world. Krispo claimed strappingly that in the past there were no selfies, and it was common for people to possess only one or two photos over the span of their entire life.

Tintypes, now they were tragically romantic.

It was particularly hard to believe that Krispo used the words *current* and *two photos* in the same explanation. It was supremely obvious that Krispo herself didn't live in the modern world.

Ugh. Selfie.

All this reminiscing stressed her. She was on the verge of a big change; she could tell.

That's what was amazing about all this. Tulip was being adolescently ironic. The kind of irony when you're pretty sure you have it nailed down—what irony is. Yet, you're still not 100 percent sure. Maybe. You might not try to explain it out loud.

In college after she graduated with a degree in philosophy and ideology, she would be able to look back and explain it perfectly. Just how ironic she was. Someday Sylvia would be big.

At midnight each day she thought about her next day, long and hard. She had many goals, and those were her moments to ponder them. Who would she be and what would she do? Tomorrow... she would see.

Selfie.

The Coworker

Her
Her past
Him
His past

It was before lunch on Monday morning when there was a knock on my office door. With all this reorganization, it was probably just another transfer from accounting or human resources, distracting me from the pile of work on my desk. The door opened, and my boss stepped in. With one last glance at my computer screen, I turned towards the open door. The wide smile of my boss, and behind him, there he stood. My mental processes stopped. I stood up and walked towards the man. Although I couldn't put the pieces of emotion together in my head, my body didn't fumble. I stuck out my hand, hoping desperately to God that he wouldn't take it. He did.

The Coworker

Introductions were being made, but they were not necessary. He was tall, taller than I had remembered, with caramel-colored eyes that seemed to be melting by the second. His jaw was square and matched the right angle of his cheek bone. It should have been a strong face, but it wasn't. He seemed timid, maybe lost; whatever his disposition, I knew exactly what he was thinking... How could this be happening after so many years?

I was standing in the kitchen next to my mother, the clank and whoosh of the dishwasher sounding steadily behind me like the steady drumbeat of an approaching execution squad. I hadn't wanted him to come. I told my mother that if he came, I would lock myself in my room. The fuss I made, you would think I was eight, but I think I was around fifteen. I was old enough to date and old enough to be a little self-conscious about the fact that I had never kissed a boy. I was also old enough to know that I was not interested in anyone my mother introduced me to.

In the end, of course he did come, and to top it off, he arrived early and caught me off guard. I was still wiping the lunch table with the bright green sponge when I heard the door click shut. I'm not even sure who let him in. He probably let himself in, really. He was always impulsive and a bit overconfident, like he was privileged for some reason.

I suddenly realized that my supervisor was still talking to me, explaining both of our positions and how we would be interacting frequently from now on.

I started to wonder which one of us would resign first.

On my first day of work after transferring from human resources, I arrived late, barely managing to grab a tie before I caught the bus heading down Harden. I spent the morning meeting dozens of new people, knowing all along that I could hardly remember the name of my sister's boyfriend, let alone everyone on the second floor of building B. After a morning that seemed to last an eternity, we were at the end of the hall ready to meet the last of my new colleagues. My new supervisor rapped on the office door and then pushed it open, not even listening for permission to enter. A brown-haired woman sat at the computer working, her head leaning intently towards the screen, observably annoyed that we had walked in without permission.

Somehow, I didn't see it coming until we were already hand in hand. Our hands grasped in a business handshake, she lifted her Bette Davis eyes and looked right into me. It was just as horrible as I thought it would be. Just as horrible, and just as wonderful; and just like that, I was right back where it all started...

I was standing on the lawn in my athletic sandals, the freshly cut grass sticking to my feet.

Glancing in the window, I saw her standing at the kitchen sink, scooping up handfuls of suds from the abundance of dish soap she had obviously put in the sink. I hadn't meant to look in the window. I was just cutting across the lawn, annoyed that my mother had arranged for me to help out this woman. An old friend, she had said, and like always, "She has a lovely daughter."

As she scooped up another mound of tiny bubbles with both hands, I heard a call from inside the house, and the girl jerked her head towards the door behind her. The window was a few inches open, and the faded yellow panes perfectly framed her head, tipping back playfully, her shaggy, short, brown hair brushing the smooth tan of her neck. I heard her call back, "Yes, Mother..." just as she cranked the water on full and lifted the bottle of dish soap high over the sink and squeezed; the long stream piercing through the already present mountain of foam. I watched her bend forward and lean into the sink, reaching into the soapy water past her elbows so that I could no longer see her whole face. Then there was a puff as she blew through the bubbles, creating a valley of suds that framed her sunburned cheeks. She really was lovely, I thought. Suddenly I was very aware of the crooked smile on my face and the flushed color of my cheeks. Here I was, standing on her lawn staring in the window, my wet feet covered in soggy grass. I couldn't meet her like this. I continued to the front door and pondered the idea of sneaking in to wash my feet. It seemed to be a fairly big house, and if I could hear her mother out the kitchen window on the other side, she probably wasn't near the front door.

Never having been this impulsive in my life, I slipped in the front door and found a bathroom immediately to my left. Thank goodness for the ranch house half-bath right inside the front door. I quickly washed my feet and legs and smoothed my hair. I opened the bathroom door to head back outside to ring the bell and ran smack into her mother.

"You're here already! Great!" she cried.

Wow, that was easy. I followed her into the kitchen, where her daughter stood wiping the table with a neon green sponge.

"Look who's here, Honey!" said her mother in a singsong voice.

I smiled at her feather light hair as she spun around to glare at me.

"I didn't hear the doorbell ring," she demanded. "Who let you in?"

"Now, dear, that is no way to talk to your new friend, is it?" The girl immediately moved her glare to her mother, who stood glowing next to her. It seemed that her mother was as subtle in her matchmaking as mine was. As she turned from her mother and walked back to the sink, I caught her eye and rolled mine, hoping that she would understand that we were on the same side. She must have understood, because the next time she glanced up at me the glare was gone and only a curious squint remained in its place.

Her mother turned and left the kitchen, murmuring something about needing to change the laundry, and left us standing there alone. I took a step forward and stuck out my hand, "Hi, new friend."

She laughed, and smiled at me with the sweetest blue eyes I had ever seen.

I came back to reality to hear my supervisor just finishing his spiel about our company restructuring. Though I couldn't be sure of what he had just said, I was fairly certain it meant that we would be working together fairly often from

now on. I should just quit now, I instinctively thought. Now standing here, hand in hand, I never thought it would be like this again; I never dreamt it. But then again, I had not allowed myself to dream of her.

Well, this is it, I thought. My work life is now officially a living hell. I mechanically followed my boss's instructions and invited the man to sit at the extra table in my tiny office. I got out the binder of protocol, prepared to drone about the proper way to prepare a report for the remaining hour before lunch. I removed an itemized form from the binder and slid it across the table to him without glancing up. Straight away, I proceeded to snap the rings of the binder shut on my finger.

"Ouch! Shit!"

Before I could stop myself, I had looked up to see him holding back a smile. I had longed for that smile.

Shit—I should be more angry. He doesn't know what happened! He knew I was pregnant and he still left. He still left, and without saying anything.

He could have gone to USC and been with me. He could have taken care of me and still gone to college. But he couldn't handle it. There were too many people who told him to get out—that it was over and there was no going back. No going back and no holding on. So that's what he did. He just got on with his life, and left me there. Still 17, still in high school, and still pregnant. He just left.

I had gone to the clinic to take the test alone—well, not completely alone—I had gone with my most sketchy friend, the only one who knew where the center was located and wasn't too nervous to go because she might be seen there. But it wasn't her I needed that day; it was him. He didn't know then. Even now, he doesn't know whether I had an abortion, or gave it up for adoption, or miscarried, or if I have a child now.

Still. He still doesn't know.

My first day in the new office, and already I just wanted out. It was just my luck that my new partner at work would end up being the only person I had ever fallen in love with. Snapping her finger in a binder, it was just so... Her.

The last time I had seen her we were sitting on a park bench next to a statue of Kirkman Finlay, the sound of the river filling the silence that foretold the end of us. We always sat next to Finlay, so we could talk in silence without anyone else copping a squat on the bench and chirping about the weather. It was kind of peaceful, really. I guess you could say we spent a fair amount of our relationship flirting and

dreaming next to a bronze statue of the former mayor.

She had been pregnant then, and I don't even know what happened. I hadn't stayed to find out. I hadn't helped, I just left. I got as far away as I could, and pretended it had ended like any other young romance.

I still don't know what happened. I protected myself from the hurt and from the guilt all those years—to the extent that I didn't allow myself to wonder. I didn't give myself even a second to imagine what she was feeling. I was unable to handle it, that's why. I would have hurt too much, so I didn't allow myself.

I glanced over at her, knowing that I would never make use of the formulas that she was now explaining. Her brown hair was still shaggy and light. I was kind of glad that it hung over her eyes when she leaned forward. It gave me a free pass to gaze at her. Her thin, tan neck and small shoulders, clenched with nervousness and stress, or maybe anger. I'm sure she wasn't happy to see me. I wonder if she still uses too much dish soap.

Six years at this company and this is how it ends. After a talk with my boss, I gathered my belongings and headed towards the back door. When I told him I needed to explore other opportunities, he gave me an inquisitive look, but said he understood all the same. I exited the building and trudged slowly down the steps towards the river. I might as well have one last sit. I sighed as I realized there was already someone there, sitting on my bench, leaning on a white cardboard file box identical to the one propped under my arm. I walked around the opposite side of the bench.

"This is my bench," I said without thinking.

"I'm so sorry," he said, looking up at me.

I looked down at his bare feet and suddenly felt like my legs could no longer hold me. I crumpled down on the bench and looked sideways at the only man I'd ever loved, nearly the father of my child, my ex-coworker.

He looked over at me with his caramel eyes, still timid, still lost.

"I hate it when wet grass sticks to my feet," he whispered.

"Your feet aren't wet anymore," I responded.

He moved his hand from his white cardboard box to mine, and set it on top of my hand. I sighed, not sure if I could even remember what happened anymore.

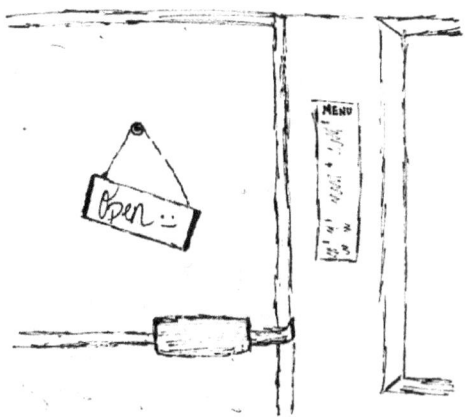

Cafe Closed

The café did not open until six each morning, but Samantha was always there at five. Even in the winter months, when the wind was so sharp and cold it seemed to etch a sharp grimace on her face. Her shoulders hunched and shook from the cold, but she didn't mind; she almost preferred it. She relished the moments when her body had to work a bit to survive. At least her mind was distracted, and she did not have to think. She had no decisions to make, only survive.

She left her house each morning at 4:40. After locking the door, she took the three front steps carefully, one at a time, right foot, together, right foot, together. They were icy in the winter, and when they were not coated with ice, chunks of cement broke off and tumbled down on the cracked sidewalk below. Three simple steps, so many problems.

At the bottom of the steps, she paused, looking down Cedar Street towards the lonely center of town. She had lived here her whole life, but she was a stranger, not unknown, but not known. She walked alone early in the morning when the city was void of traffic and human interaction, unsure whether she did it by choice or by necessity. She turned right and started the steep climb up Barck Street, methodically noticing the variation in the shoveling of the sidewalk at the border of each yard. At the corner of Barck and Elm she paused, as if patiently waiting for the light to change and the traffic to stop. But there was no red light, nor was there any traffic, just the blinking yellow of the caution light, reminding her that she was indeed alone. She always waited an extra minute or two. She paused an extra moment longer today, just to let time pass, and for another reason too. There was a co-op gas station on the corner that was already open, and some days, she could see her sister there, stocking the shelves or doing bookwork.

She was always early too. Their father had raised them like that. He was always on time. Always drunk, but always on time. Her sister never saw her, standing there on the corner, looking sideways through the frosty and smudged windows. Or maybe she did, Samantha was sure that even if her sister did see her, she would never have shown any sign of it. Her sister did not think much of her, after all.

For years Samantha had been waiting it out, hoping Jen would forgive her, or at least acknowledge her. She had no other reason to stay in this town. The sunrise shift at the worn out café, the square block two-bedroom house where she lived that never changed on the outside, and on the inside, became lonelier and more discouraging with each passing year; it was all worth nothing. She had nothing, and there was nothing here for her.

It had been her grandfather's house until he died, then it had become hers, not because she bought it, but because no one else wanted it, and because she had nowhere else to go. The last person in her family that she had spoken to was her grandfather, which reminded her how long it had really been.

She didn't know where their mother was. She worked, so she may have been there, but that didn't seem right. She was like Jen. No drinking, but an underlying current of pride. Pride and antipathy. They would never do what she had done. Her mother and her sister, both, were above it all. Above the bad choices, above the genes.

Good genes, bad genes.

Family is family, her mother had always said, so many exceptions though. Family is family when you were following the rules—for the most part. The double standard was another exception. Samantha knew her mother had at least one affair. She didn't blame her really. No one's perfect. Plus, her father had a lover on the side as well, it was just that his mistress came in a glass bottle with a price tag and smelled like juniper or peat, depending on the darkness of a particular night.

What a terrible family tree she could have drawn. One nuclear family, 4 square, with offshoots of gnarled vines, overlapping sinisterly around each branch. Only Jen's would be bare, except that the abuse she had endured over the years left her branch undersized and malnourished. It was so weak and desperately in need of stability. Gentle breezes traumatized it, and every night, every day, of her life was fraught with storms of lightning and thunder. No support came from the trunk, simply a physical connection of parent to child, sister to sister.

Oh, she missed Jen.

And a burn down the side of the trunk where the constant drip, drip of grain alcohol had worn away the protective bark of love that you would normally find on a family tree.

She shivered. How cruel this disease was.

When they were old enough to realize what was happening, together they made a plan. As 14-year-olds, they researched alcoholism, primarily via a set of dark blue World Book Encyclopedias at the public library. They'd looked up cirrhosis and alcohol hepatitis. Jen had drawn a diagram of the human body with notes on the health problems most often associated with drinking and labeled them with rankings from most to least harmful, short term and long term symptoms and side effects. The silhouette of the diagram bore a striking resemblance to their father.

Samantha shivered again. When Jen drew a diagram for her own children, it would have shoulder length brown hair pulled back into a low ponytail, small shoulders long hunched from the cold, and slim feet. Because of the things she had done for so many years, just like her father had.

Jen started drinking in high school, just casually with friends. Sometimes Samantha joined, but she felt uneasy about it, almost as if she had a premonition, as if their father weren't reason enough. As a 16-year-old, awareness of presentiment is rare, however, and by the time Jen got married, Samantha was so deep she should have been drawing her own diagram.

She failed out of college, and moved back home, or more accurately, she had Jen drive to MSU and pick up her belongings from her shitty sophomore year apartment. Samantha was already back in their hometown, living half at her boyfriend's apartment and spending the remaining half at Jen and Paul's, or her grandpa's, occasionally.

She had gotten his genes, and at that point, she was sure she had no chance. There was no amount of love or hard work that could help her get through it. Her blood, her brain, and her very soul were drawn to drunkenness.

Yes, that's how bad it was.

It's over, she had said to Jen one night, I'm him, and there's nothing I can do about it. I'm as good as dead. She'd had 18 drinks that night. The bartender had given her the tab the next morning.

When she was back there at 11:13 a.m.

The words her sister had spoken that night stayed with her, and still stuck in her throat, trying to make their way down to her heart or up into her brain. Fighting, fighting.

You can beat this, Sam.

She was 26.

Twelve years later and she had now been sober for eight years. She had gone to work every day for eight years.

Every. Single. Day.

She had found no other way to stay away from it, her one true love, except to work herself to the bone. She now made the schedule, and opened at six thirty, but actually started at five. She worked 5 hours and 43 minutes on the clock every day of the week. The owner didn't mind this strange set up, he sensed that something was off with Samantha, that something about her was irregular. When she clocked out at 12:13 every day, she stayed at the café. She cleaned, she rolled silverware, she chatted with regulars, she buffed the counter to a sheen. No one minded. She was a very good worker.

On the anniversary of her eighth sober year, she'd gone to the gas station to tell Jen.

There was nothing more that Samantha wanted than her sister. *You can beat this, Sam.* She longed for Jen's sisterly devotion, but it had worn well away in the four years it took for her to hit rock bottom. Ow. The bottom of life was so hard.

She went right at 6 to tell her, but Jen kept the door locked. 6:15, 6:30. How were there no customers? Fate was cruel, that was the truth. Eventually Sam had moved on down the street. The frozen tears were burning roughly in the corners of her eyes. It was what she deserved.

That day she had gone to the bar. The pain had pulled her there, gripping at her wrist, her right palm tingling in anticipation of a sweating glass in her hand. She walked through the front door and stepped into the aroma of her dreams. She'd made so many mistakes, and here she was again, fighting the devil while holding his hand. It was unclear what made her turn around and go back out the door. The memories, perhaps? Or the hope of looking into her sister's smiling eyes? The nausea of living at the point of no return, too drunk to make it back to sobriety before sleep took her. Sleep. The only way back to light for a decade.

Logic? Horror? Pain? Something led her back out the door and to work. She apologized for arriving so late and went right to the sink. She scrubbed and scrubbed. Their father had been right about that. Cleaning, busy hands, working, busy feet, busy mind, a tired mind. It was the only way he could keep to it. He died anyway, of complications of the liver and the heart, and the stomach. That much liquor just wore you away over time. Samantha knew about this. She had strange hurts, forgetful moments that didn't quite seem natural. Aging didn't cut that deep that fast.

Samantha worked, Jen lived, and maybe one day they would speak again.

Tomorrow was nine years, and Samantha had decided to try again. The day before, she had seen Jen's son at the park on her way home from work. She saw her sister's cheekbones and her own chin, and it hurt her more than the drink had. She wasn't even sure of his name, but she was sure it was him. A sort of pride burst through her. The feeling was so warm that she had sighed in relief. It was life, rolling through her veins and arteries. She had to know this little boy.

Tomorrow she would take a lunch break for the first time in a long, long time. She would go see Jen. She would find her at the register, or better yet, they would meet in the aisle.

She would look up into Jen's hazel eyes, identical to her own. "You don't have to punish me," she would plead, if she could conjure the words. "My life is punishment enough." She shivered when she imagined the burning look on her sister's face, bitter and angry, so disgusted to be speaking with her. "You don't know what it's like," she would continue, "to be the one who followed in his footsteps." She felt a choke in her throat imagining the two of them side by side, father and daughter, "when it was so horrible, and you were able to escape," she would finish. Their green eyes connected would start to swim as they glistened with the slightest moisture of tears. She could go on, but there would be no need. They both knew how he was, and they really didn't need a reminder of it.

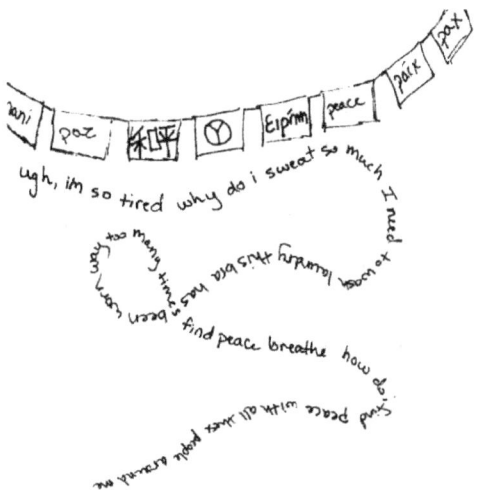

Unyoga

In a yoga studio, a dozen people sit cross-legged or in lotus, one in half-lotus, waiting for a class to begin. A sign on the door reads "Prana: Donation Based Yoga   5:30 Monday." *Monday* has been crossed out, and *TODAY* has been written above it.

The instructor is speaking over soft meditation music, repeating the calm-inducing words that begin every class.

"Simply let your thoughts flow in and out."

At her last word, we fly swiftly into her mind and see a meadow and a waterfall.

Along the waterfall, a man walks with a young child, and also a woman. We soon realize through the flashes of her memories that the child is her daughter, the man, her husband, and the woman, his new wife.

This is her daughter's new family. We feel longing and pain. We hear laughter and see tears. She remembers her daughter's birth, her first steps, a temper tantrum, a new teddy bear. It fades and washes away, back to the present.

We view the class. There are three rows of three and one lone woman in the fourth row. Inhalation through exhalation, we move slowly through each student in the class, one scene, then a split scene, then four, then nine. We see office work, promotions, lunch, lovers fighting, and lovers making up. Sometimes the lovers overlap. As we reach the forced tranquility on the face of the last person in the room, there is a whisper of something in the air. She is the new wife. In the mind's eye of the woman, we see the same meadow, the same waterfall. Walking along the waterfall is the man and the little girl. Walking with them is a woman, but it's not her, it's the yoga instructor. We fade far away as the class ends, two identical waterfalls, festering in the minds of both women.

Savasana.

The Argentinean Champagne Heist

All heists start with a conman, and that is me. Everything I do, everything I say, I am a quintessential, half Russian, half Italian mafia capitalist. A non-discriminating riskist. My mother would so not be proud.

Ha! Actually, my mother is so very proud, because she taught me everything that I know! My dear mama would be Conwoman of the Year if there were such a title. She'd win it every year and swipe the prize money from the hosts before they had a chance to award it to her. This is likely why they don't have such an award. Oh, cons. You've got to love them.

I've had many a good heist in my prolifically naughty days, but my hundredth, the so-called Argentinean Champagne Heist, will be the best of all.

I came, I seized, I slipped away. I can hear the commendations coming in already!

The plan is superficially simple. I can sum it up in very few words: Blissful, bubbly, betrayal.

This, my mother will be proud of, or at least I very much hope so, because it's all for her.

One thousand bottles of bubbly dubbly champagne for my mama, that's what a real conman would do. How often does an old broad turn 60, anyway?!

Once, that's how often.

In 30 days it would be my mama's birthday, and she's the best of them all, so how could I not plan something fan-fucking-tacular for her!?

It wouldn't really be Argentinean. Hell! Does Argentina even grow champagne? Likely not.

But it would be foreign enough, this tiny Panamanian vineyard that made the perfect *blubbly* pink for my old ma. Special, but hardly special enough for the mama that taught me everything I know.

I had a team of three. Two were my old comrades from Port Costa School. The very place where all my tricks began! The third was hand-picked by me and given the nod by mi mamá. Ooold Stabbing Joe was the best in the biz after my mother (and perhaps yours truly, but I shall be modest), but then something terribly awful happened and OSJ lost an eye and a hand.

Shucks. That's how I feel about that. Just awww, shucks. It's painful to lose an eye, even if you are doing what you love.

I couldn't wait for the party. This grand ole shindig! There would be cold shrimp and hot barbequed cocktail wienies! I'd have oranges picked from our tree in Fresno and a chocolate fountain. We'd dip and drizzle all sorts of things: fat white marshmallows and half peeled bananas. Colorful, freshly-made cake pops (I found those on Pinterest—chock full of ideas, a conman's dream!), and last but not least… those Babybels. Yum. My ma put a tiny net of them in my lunch box every Monday, age 5 to 35.

I wanted one of those champagne fountains too, thus the need for the load of stolen champagne, and if all went well, we would have it. I would pop the cork and poooooour! Mommy dear would love it!

Once my team was assembled, I got right down to business. Old S. Joe would be my right hand man. He had more experience than me if the truth be told, so I'd be able to count on him. He would also drive the getaway car. Or more like, getaway truck!

Operation Champagne Heist began with a fake rush order of 100 cases. 10 bottles per case and that's a thousand! And what is special about this order, why it's champagne to be picked up rather than delivered. Ahh, yes. It 'tis.

My fake name was all set and sorted out, Johan Brother Grimm. Quite a handsome name, I might add.

I would arrange the date and time for pick up, and have a bill sent to the false identity at a post office box of my choosing.

When the bill came, I would rip it to pieces and never pay! Ha! A grand Ha!

By the time they realized I'd swiped the wool right in front of their eyes, the champagne would be drunk, and the red SOLO cups would be long cleared.

They could send the bills again and again, yet I would never know and never respond.

It was ingenious! Smooth assed brother Johan would have that post office box for life for all I cared!

The day came, and we made the trip south. We flew from Fresno to LAX, LAX to Houston, Houston to Panama City and there in The City, 3rd in command, Bobby G rented a truck. He picked us up at the airport—obvs, he had flown ahead. Timing! Timing is everything!

The trip to the champagne farm took 3 hours and 20 minutes exactly. I was nervous every second, biting my mama-packed carrot sticks rather than my fingernails. She thought I was off to D-land for the day! What a trick! I do love me some Space Mountain.

When we arrived, it was full tilted time. We hustled and bustled like it was the end of the world, and in no time at all we had every case of champagne loaded onto the truck.

Next was the long drive. We drove that champagne from country to country, crossing border after dangerous border. OSJ took care of every one of them. As I said, my mumsy taught him everything that he knows. When we crossed the Tijuana border successfully I hooted and hollered. "Hells yeah, Old Stabbing Joe! You do good work!"

In truth, I had been worried about that one. In other countries, you have to ease and wedge and connive, but in the U.S. of A, why, that's a wee bit more difficult. But we were back and in a mirror 5 hours and 26 minutes we were at the warehouse back home, getting' tha' there champagne chillin.'

We'd made it!

I had ice at the ready. My man number 3 made sure of that. We crushed and we slammed and all 1,000 bottles were golden before long.

The party was in 10 short hours.

I went to sleep just in time, my mother fast asleep in the next bedroom. I marveled at the wonder that was in store for her the next day, my dear mama.

The party went off without a hitch pin. We talked and laughed and sang, we dipped our fingers in chocolate, we gambled, we danced. We drank a champagne fountain that was worthy of my mother and only her.

Deep into the morning after the long night, I walked my mama back to the house from the old field of fun. The bonfire was still burning and my team still celebrating their success.

In our kitchen, she continued on to brush her teeth, she always was a rule oriented one, my ma. While she did, I took the extra step and began to wash the marshmallow plates. As I dried them and put them away in the special dish cupboard, a long roll of receipts fell out.

To my utter shock and awe, at the top was the name of the very champagne farm that I'd chosen.

A bill. It was a bill. How had they found me!?

And a payment date! My God, what had happened!?

"Mama!" I hollered. "What is this!?" I held up the long, itemized receipt for one thousand bottles of … "Ahh, Mama! Jeepers creepers, you even paid the import tax! How could you!?"

My mama made her way slowly back into the dining room. She turned up the dimmer and then came towards me, putting both hands on my cheeks, which were flushed from the warmth of the giant bonfire.

"Oh, honey," she said, "yous not a con."

I stared and my jaw dropped slack.

"Darlin,' I've been tiptoeing around your labors since you first tampered with your opponent's boxcar derby car."

"Mama, no!"

"You were so proud of greasing the axle of that little car, but you made it far better than it had been. It would have won in a heartbeat! I *had* to just up and super glue the back axle at the last minute! Thank goodness I had my destroyer kit along."

"But mama!"

"It's ok, dear, I love you, you know?"

"But mama, I did it all for you!"

"Well, I know that honey. I did it all for you too. By the way son, this here stunt you just pulled—doing the marshmallow plates and finding my receipt stash? Why that is the sneakiest, most unexpected stunt you have ever accomplished. Congrats!"

"Oh, Mama," I smiled. "I love ya so."

"Love you too, son. Love you too."

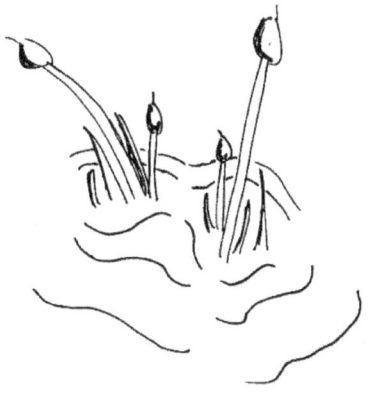

The Cattails

He looked down at his hands, stained permanently with ink from the many years spent working at the press. He retired early, after almost four decades of work.

He was a good husband; devoted, kind, caring; and he was a wonderful father; careful, understanding, teaching. They had three children and were happily married. They could not finish each other's sentences, they were not that kind of a couple, but when making necessary or critical household decisions, she could make them without him, and he without her. They knew what they wanted in life.

She was going to work a few years longer than he had. They had agreed it would be better if he moved out to the old cabin right away. He could have his peace there. It was more of an old boat shed, really.

He had converted it into a little cabin piece by piece on their many trips there over the years. The boathouse was the peace that he needed. All those years of compressed, rushed life—now they needed to be released, pondered.

He used to fish, but he was too old now. It was too hard to be up or to walk down to the water, even without carrying his old wooden pole and tackle box, so he just sat. His chair faced the window so he could look out towards the water and watch the reeds and cattails at the water's edge as they swayed in the breeze. The lake supplied a lot of the water for the city, so with the recent years' population increase, the edge of the water was slowly receding. At first it made him sad, thinking about the beautiful lake, slowly receding. But now, it was just another sign of the passage of time.

He had always pictured these last few moments in his mind. They would be sitting by the window, staring out at the lake and the overgrown reeds. Maybe they would be holding hands, like an old romance film. They would pass on peacefully, there together at the boathouse. He now considered that her vision was probably quite similar; they were sitting together by the window, looking out. Only the location was different. In her vision, perhaps they were looking out the white paned window that looked down Cedar Street, watching the city pass by, glancing at the driveway where they had played basketball with their boys, where Anne had ridden her tricycle in circles. Funny how decades together never brought up the question of where they would be when their lives ended. Years living happily together, and it was never brought up, only assumed that it was together. It was clear now that it wasn't. Now that they were here in this time, it seemed even those same decades together could not change their minds. Some paths simply couldn't be altered.

She wanted to stay and work in the city for a few more years. She liked working and the city life of lights and people. The big old house in the city was full of memories of their life together, their work, their children, their marriage, even their old cocker spaniel, Lucy. She loved the memories that flooded over her each time she opened the door. When she retired, they could live the rest of their lives together. Until then, they would visit and spend weekends together.

It seemed now that he had been waiting a long time. She had said she would see him soon. He wondered now if she had been referring to him going into the city. He loved her so much, but he was just too old to chase, to argue, maybe even to visit. Over the last few years, this had become his home and his life. He could not imagine changing it now. He looked out at the reeds and cattails outside his window, barely swaying in the fall drafts. It had been years now.

She returned home from the clinic each day using the same route. First, a short ride on bus 101, no more than fifteen minutes; where she would pass the bakery, the smell of fresh bread wafting through the bus windows as they slowed to turn left; and then the children's book store, where she had picked out gifts for her three children throughout the years. Just before her stop, they passed the Polish deli, where, for years, she had purchased meat to make sandwiches for her family's lunches. She got off at the corner of Cedar and Winston, and then walked two blocks uphill towards her house, where her cat, Ricky, sat on her windowsill and waved its tail in the white paned window. She could see him welcoming her home each day, waiting for her company.

She had not meant for it to end this way. Her retirement paperwork was complete, but still sitting on her desk next to the old piano. She was still not ready to turn it in. She felt a pang of guilt. How long had it been?

She decided to drive up to the lake that night. It really had been too long. When she opened the door to the old cabin with her square, tarnished key, she felt a rush of warm air. She walked into the kitchen and looked around. A bowl and spoon sat in the sink. He ate oatmeal every morning, oatmeal with bananas and brown sugar, and orange juice. There was no juice glass in the sink. When she was not around he always drank the juice straight out of the carton.

She turned left towards a short hallway that led towards the main room. The living room, the den, the four seasons room, this was his room. He ate here, he slept here, he read here, and if they ever talked on the phone, he was here, sitting in his worn, flowered brown chair. As she entered the room, she could see him sitting there now, in his chair. She paused, noticing the dark lamp shade. She knew then. She knew from the many years they lived together that he always turned on the lamp at dinner. It was long past dinner, and he was still sitting in front of the window, staring out at the dark, as if watching the water slowly receding. It had once been so beautiful.

She wondered how long he had been like this, alone. It could not have been too long. The house still smelled like oatmeal and aftershave, nothing more. She felt remorse. Not necessarily for not being with him when he died, but for not realizing that this is how it would end. For not seeing the angle of their paths, so parallel when they began their life together. All along, they had made the same choices, raised a wonderful family, and built a home. They had made all the correct and intelligent budget decisions, saving appropriately for life after retirement. But now, when it was really their time to be together, to rest; for the first time, they chose differently, and for the first time, they did not even realize their divergence.

There must have been a fork in the road. She thought back, but could not remember.

The plan had clearly been to wait together. To pass the time until they reached their final resting place, together. They were young when they were married. They moved away from their families and found a place of their own. Then, still young, they had children; so that later, after they retired, they could be together. To read, relax, and reminisce; at least that is what they had thought. She could not remember now. Had there been a plan? Or had their family been it?

She turned and left the room. She shut off the light in the hall, and then the light in the kitchen. She locked the door behind her with her square, tarnished gold key. She would call the children first. They were most important. Later, she would take care of the rest. She got in her car and turned to drive back to the city, knowing that she would never return to the boat house.

Pozole, because rain
A Story of Loss

Good morning! On this fresh Monday morning I'd like to take a moment to introduce you to someone special. Our guest today is nationally-renowned for her spectacular culinary skills. After a life-changing disease entered her life and altered all that she knew and loved, this young woman took life by the reins and turned to

the kitchen and a set of
well-sharpened   cutlery.
Over the past five years,
she has become one of the
most intriguing members of
the modern culinary field.
With fresh ingredients and
fresh ideas, in no time at
all she moved forward and
into   an   absolutely
astonishing career. Ladies
and gentlemen, Ms. Jennifer
Laysen is here with us this
morning. Please give her a
warm welcome.
Welcome to the studio, Ms.
Laysen! It's a pleasure to
have you. You've got so
much going on and with such
an amazing story. It was
almost impossible to get
you booked on the show; you
are simply too busy! How do
you keep it all straight
nowadays!?

Thank you so much. It's my
pleasure to be here, and
yes! It is, at times, quite
difficult to keep it all
straight.   I   now   have

engagements almost every week and that's on top of my cooking and baking!

Is it difficult? To maintain a lifestyle at this speed in your current condition? It isn't every day you find a woman in the public eye—working and constantly giving interviews, plus a chef—who has multiple sclerosis. How is it that you do it all?

Well, I manage to make do somehow. You see, as a child I was very, very active. I hiked, went mountain biking—I went hang gliding the second that I was old enough. I still have all that energy, but I put it towards other purposes. I cook, I talk, ha! I think; I plan.

What a busy woman. And how did you end up being a chef?

Well, I actually came from a family of chefs.

Uhhuh. Go on, please.

My mom seemed to be a little relieved when it all came down to it and I had nowhere else to turn but cooking with fresh vegetables and herbs.

Relieved?

Um, not relieved.

I see. I apologize, do go on.

Well, heh, outdoor adventures aren't a career. My mother always knew that; I didn't, I readily admit.

Hm. I understand… And what happened next? Would you mind sharing a little more?

Next?

Yes.

Or before that?

Yes.

When I was just five years old they already called me a tomboy.

Oh?

I was climbing trees, jumping off the swing from the highest point; my mother just couldn't keep me at home.

Did you ever cook when you were young?

No, not really. Hahah! I was too busy playing!

Really? So how is it that you learned your craft? At what moment did you begin to harness your talent?

Hmm... Harness my craft, that's a tough one. I, I... ...It all started one day. I had a back spasm.

Pozole, because rain

A back spasm?

Yes. It was weird and tingly and so… painful, I guess.

That must have been difficult.

It was. I was only 16.

Yes, of course. Ms. Laysen, do you find that what happened when you were so young shaped who you are— who you have become?

Call me Jen, please.

Jen, thank you.

Of course. I was just such an active young woman. So on the go! How could I not be changed dramatically after my body… after… losing the use of my legs.

I'm so sorry. That must have been so difficult. If

I might ask, you have no feeling in your legs today?

Feeling? Some days yes, some days, no. But you see, when I was young I had so much fun going out and exploring nature and national forests and parks, meadows, skydiving and stargazing and jumping off waterfalls. I was quite the daredevil, actually. I climbed a 14,000-ft peak once.

I do believe I read that once.

Oh, yes, of course. Was it in *The American Athlete*?

Excuse me?

The article where you read that? Was it in *The American Athlete*?

Perhaps. That could be it. Is that important to you?

Uh, I was interviewed by them once for National MS Month… about Mount Evans. That was truly one of my best climbs ever. I did it alone, so they loved hearing my story. Some say it was risky, but that's me I guess. Ha! A madcap adventurer!

Do you enjoy giving interviews? You have such a spirited personality.

I do like giving interviews. It lets me tell my story, which I think is important. When you're such an energetic and athletic person like I was, and you are so unfortunate as to contract a debilitating disease such as MS, it's important to be able to share—to let out all the—the…

The feelings?

Um, I mean—yes, of course the feelings, but more… about me, about the change, I guess. It didn't change who I was, you know. Don't you think it's amazing for people, the average person, at least, to be able to talk to someone like me?

Yes, of course.

Yes.

If I might shift the conversation to your career…

Yes, of course. Go ahead. I'll answer anything.

What are your future plans in the kitchen?

You see I'm very accustomed to getting questions about everything that I've been through. Hahuaha! I'll answer pretty much anything at this point.

Pozole, because rain

Are you planning anything
special for the next year?

Yes, yes of course, because
the past is the future,
isn't it?

Why, yes it is. Did I hear
a little something about
television?

I don't watch a lot of
television, in fact. I've
always been, in the past
you know, more interested
in getting out, talking to
the people, being in "the
world"! That's how I see
it.

Is it true that you've been
working with WFS on a new
program?

Yes! That is true. Welcome
Family Studios will be
producing my new series.

Wonderful. Congratulations.
Could you tell us a little
more about it?

Yes, it's a family show which will be called, "Eat, Live, Go."

And what kind of dishes will you be preparing on the show?

Many, many dishes. It will be the perfect show for the person on the go-the family on the go, more like. You might think that's funny, right? Considering my current, uh, but I was always so full of energy that I remember it like a glove. Back in the old days I could hardly sit down to eat! I didn't, usually; I was just running to and fro to events and competitions and trips with a peanut butter and jelly sandwich.

Can you give us a little taste, pardon the pun, of what you'll be preparing on the show?
Well, for starters, a peanut butter and jelly

sandwich! Hahhhehheee! Oh, the curveballs life throws us, eh?

Yes, so many curveballs. And have you begun filming? Would you mind sharing a little about the process for our viewers today?

Certainly, certainly. The studio, Welcome Family Studios, has been great about making accommodations. There's a very modern commercial kitchen, of course, and also, what's really amazing is that behind the cooking island is a photographic display, a sort of collage of photos of my life before. It's really a great project. There's a graphic designer working on it with me and she had some really innovative ideas in terms of design that will very artistically and poetically show how *who I was* isn't lost. It's still a part of me, a rather large and important part of me.

Certainly. Yes, of course. In terms of the series, what kind of culinary treats do you have in store for us? Will the episodes be thematic? Regional? What are your thoughts on the food?

Oh, yes. I've got some great ideas. You see, back in the day, I took a high school trip to Namibia. I went on a lot of great hikes, and on one in particular, a full-day hike down to the ocean, I traversed through a very interesting village. There they had the most interesting cuisine. I'm planning to work more with the inspiration I collected on that trip. Perhaps I'll even make a trip back! Speaking of culturally diverse culinary treats, one of your most famous

dishes is a certain type of
Mexican soup, I believe.

Yes, that's true. The first
soup that I, personally,
ever made was a pozole.

Pozole. And why pozole?

Pozole. Well, to be frank,
it was the first day…

The first day…?

The, the first day of the,
the end. I guess…

The end. Would you tell us
more?

…

If you don't mind.

…I had a back spasm. A bad
one. And no one in my
family was home. They were
all off at work or school
or, other places. And I lay
there, on the floor,
waiting for someone to get

home. I couldn't feel my
legs at all, eventually.
But no one came, and after
hours—hours and hours—I was
hungry, so I dragged myself
to the cupboard, and pulled
out a can of hominy.

Hominy.

I found a can of hominy and
a pot. I don't know how I
reached the faucet. Maybe I
filled it with my tears.

I'm sorry.

I don't pity myself.

Of course not. You've been
so brave.

There was no one, and it
was raining.

Rain.
Rain can really affect
someone. I'd been worried,
more worried than I ever
told my parents. I was just
a kid then, a child.

I'm sure they would have understood.

Still. I didn't want to be that person.

What do you mean?

I knew it hurt more than it should. I knew that the pain was recurring far more often than it should, but I didn't say anything.

I can understand that. Do you know why you didn't say anything? Why you kept it secret?

I, I didn't want to believe it myself. I was so independent, and so active. How could I tell them that I was slowly but steadily becoming the child that they had never wanted?

Oh. What do you mean? What could that- the child that they never wanted...?

A child that was slowly regressing. I was going back in time to become a creature that needed help and support—not just mental—but also physical. Both. I'd, I, I would need them to carry me up the stairs. Down the stairs. Into the bathroom. I couldn't, at that time, be that person. I couldn't tell them that right then, at that moment when they thought all their dreams for their children were coming true, that their best and grandest daughter was going to be the one that kept them at home, year after year.

But... Jen...

No, I didn't know. However, I *did* know. One doesn't just become disabled overnight. I wasn't in a car crash. There was no accident. I was slowly

falling apart, vertebra by
vertebra. I was becoming
someone that needed
support.

I'm sure that never crossed
their-

So I made pozole. Dragged
my limp legs across the
floor and somehow—against
all odds—I managed to make
a completely and entirely
delicious batch of pozole.
I honestly don't know how I
knew what to do and what to
add. I had obviously
watched my mom cook for
years; she's a highly
skilled chef. But that
doesn't mean you actually
learn. I had the touch,
despite the fact that this
was not the life I wanted.
I wanted to be anywhere but
the kitchen, hiking,
climbing, working, scaling,
jumping, flying…

Your pozole is delicious.

Thank you so much for asking me here today.

Of course. It was wonderful to have you, and thank you so much for sharing.

Of course. I never mind sharing my story. I've had such great changes and opportunities…

As I said at the start of our interview today, it's really great to have the ability to move beyond.

Yes.

Ms. Laysen, I'd like to wish you the very best of luck with your cooking career. Motivation and great ideas, I hope you are able to make the most of this wonderful opportunity. I think it could take you far in this world.

Thank you so much.

Slices of Storm: #PCT

The storm occurred on the top of a bluff in the Sierras, not so far off the Pacific Crest Trail.

There was so much lightning. I can't even describe it.

There were fallen trees of gorgeous colors, pink, green, blue, and yellow streaked. This was so strange, likely because it was my first trip down this particular path.

The light in the sky was the iconic silhouette of the forest lands. The outlines of pine trees framed the sky from the Earth.

And the sky, well it was dark and light, red and green. It was all contrast. Just like the perfectly spread needles of each branch of each tree, reaching into the depth of the stormy red darkness of the sky.

I felt so much that night. Such absurdity, blue whales howling at the moon. The confluence of deprivation and indulgence.

The hollowness of the tree in the center of the forest called. It had been overcast, and the bolts of lightning began one by one. To the north, to the west, to the south. They surrounded us slowly. I was not alone.

Gradually, they swirled and tipped the environment, closer and closer. They encroached upon me as if entering a battle. I could not see all of them at once, nor could I understand precisely where they were advancing.

Like a synesthetic, I could see sound. The beautiful sounds and the haunting color opponents of the night sky. And it was beautiful. It kept me up all night!

Like each cell, I looked from site to site, unmoving but watching. Lightning, thunder, counting. When I'd stayed too long, it had become too much. Next was always available.

The rain came. The hail came. The wind came. It all came and climaxed in such a gloriously horribly terrifying storm. I rested.

It lightened and all was calm. A chill set in. We were downhill. Would I again be uphill?

Yes, but it was not the same. The storm was over. And it had changed me. Never had I been so close to such illuminance. The hands of gods. It might have even touched me. The electric spark of nature.

One may not know. The results of a strike are inconsistent.

Sleep never comes, not during a storm or after a storm. And before, well no, the electricity in the air changes you, makes you feel something different, something other.

The moon was later full and we all saw. Grace was there.

The effects of such a storm.

When

When it hurts too much,
I just let it roll over me
like a storm.

The pain,
it closes in.
There are no images,
no salvation, just
deep hurt.

The searing of tears to come and
a gasp,

And I know
that I have experienced loss.

The Screwtape Tales:
Possible Stories

1. There once was an internetless family.

"It doesn't matter if your iPhone doesn't work. This is a family vacation."

What did he mean by family vacation? Without internet, this was clearly a forced imprisonment. Nowadays who can go without internet?

"You know what we need, kids? We need some tunes. This radio station fuzz is ta-tripping me out! Eh? Eh? How cool is your old man? Marie, will you hand me a tape? Pick yourself out a good one, love."

"I don't have them honey, they're in the back with Salem. Salem, will you hand your dad a tape?"

I grunted a negative response, but reached down to retrieve the cardboard box below my feet. More music meant less talk.

"Which one?" I asked.

"Well there, whatcha got?"

I sighed, and began reading off names. *Cassette tapes,* these were *cassette tapes.* "Patsy Cline, Harry Connick, Jr., Garth Brooks-"

"Which Garth Brooks?"

"Ropin' the Wind." I was attempting to keep my voice as monotone and unenthusiastic as possible; that one made it hard. "David Bowie, Eagles Greatest Hits-"

"There we go! That's the winner! Bring on the Eagles! Witchy wooooooman." He sang the overplayed chorus with a howl.

Oh, this was awful.

I handed him the tape and he popped it in.

"Dad, why are we doing this?" My little brother asked. He was sweet and young, but he still understood boredom.

"Doing what, son?"

"This long drive."

"Don't you want to visit the very spot where your mom and I met?"

"No!" My brother and I shouted in unison.

"Come on! If we had never met, you wouldn't be here!"

"So?" I responded hurtfully. "Right now I wish I had never been born." I *hated* this.

"Salem!" My mother cried out. "Don't say things like that!"

"Why? I'm the shortest and dumbest girl in my class and I'm the only one not wearing a bra." At the mention of the word *bra* my father looked sharply up at the rearview mirror before shuddering and then looking down with great focus at the road ahead.

I rolled my eyes and continued, "And now I have been forced to spend my *entire* summer vacation in a car without an auxiliary jack, driving north toward the middle of nowhere when I'd rather be going south toward somewhere warm and fun."

"Oh, Salem, honey, it'll happen. Growing up takes time."

Did they hear anything I'd said?

"Why do you want boobs?" Darin asked. "Then you can't run as fast."

"Darin!" My mother and father chastised.

I couldn't help but crack a smile.

"Mom, you've got next to nothing, so I don't think I have much to look forward to."

"Salem, that's about enough. Your mother looks beautiful. Now let's change the subject."

"Thanks, honey." She gave a smile to my father. It was way too full of cheese. "Yes, now who's going to put up the tent?"

After a brief silence, I volunteered for the task of my choice. "I'll check out the restroom, shower, and host situation."

"Hey! You always do that," exclaimed Darin, "but you really just walk around."

"I can even get wood," I added. Anything to get a little air.

"You don't help get the camp set up."

"It's alright son," their father interjected. "The men will get everything set up. It's what we do!" He gave a loud, low grunt and pumped his fist in the air. Darin followed suit. I rolled my eyes again, but then Darin turned to me.

"I'll get the fire started after you get the wood!"
I nodded.

"Great, bud!" called my dad.

"Now that we've got that settled, Salem, hand me another tape. This Eagles one had a rough side A. Let's give Bowie a try. He's a mood changer."

"Young Americans?"

"Yup. Young Americans, just like you kids!"

"Oh, dad," I muttered.

"Don't 'oh, dad' me. I know! I'm wise. Someday you guys will appreciate all this, even the Eagles!"

I sighed and took the tape from over his shoulder. After handing him the new tape, I examined him for a second in the rearview mirror and then glanced over at my mother and brother before slipping the tape, unnoticed, out the cracked car window.

I'd had plenty of that for a lifetime. Ugh. I'll never be more than a b-cup.

2. "Take it to the limit," by the Eagles

Tears. Many tears. They rolled down, poured down, frolicking over my bottom lids and over my cheeks.

Cheeks emaciated from the emotion and physical pain of the last 11 months and 29 days. Or was it 30 days?

And now it was the last day.

The last day apart before we…

That's all I knew—one day to decide, never mind the fact that he had to choose as well.

It's amazing how fast a year went.

I lived a full year alone, like an average, everyday single woman in her forties. Except I wasn't. I was a married woman, and I had been married for 16 years.

It was a nice marriage, a good partnership. This past year started out with months of riding a spectrum of horrible—from shrieking, gasping solitude—and then suddenly, it just wasn't. It was different now, a completely different life altogether, not better, and not at all the same. I had survived it.

A tiny seedling, not even a seedling—a cleome—that's how this plan started. There was a job offer on the table. It was our kitchen table, and the job offer was for him.

We were discussing whether or not he should take it, but then, instead of *deciding together*, we decided that we wouldn't be together.

Somehow, over a bottle of wine—my favorite bottle of Turkovich wine—we talked our way from staying or moving, to splitting up for one year and then deciding what to do.

I was always something of a procrastinator, but this was beyond even my worst nightmares of put-offs.

What am I supposed to do!? I love my job. I like my home. I love my city.

And my husband…?   What would I decide?
What would he decide?   And what if we decided
differently? I have no idea.

Absolutely no idea.

I've heard this song a million times!

And *this* is how it ends? Fuck. I can't. I can't
take it to the limit any more, not one single time
more. Eject! Damn it! I can't decide. This is shit.
This tape is gone.

I can't decide.

3. Give me back my 8-track and I'll let you have your PONO.

"I have 27,000 songs on my phone."

"So?"

"So that's amazing. How could the present not
be better than the past?"

"That's what you want, bro?   More, more,
more?"

"Maybe.   Well, yeah.   Why not!?   With
technology the way it is, we're living the dream!"

"I don't really think this is the dream. There are so many things that are worse now than they were before."

"Like what?"

"What do you mean, 'like what?'? Think about how your parents grew up."

"What, with cholera and shit?"

"Your parents had cholera?"

"No, not exactly."

"Then think about it. Think about how they used to play in the street with the neighbor kids."

"That's what you want? Children playing in the street? Sounds unsafe to me."

"They knew their neighbors! They had enough time to plant tulips and have Sunday dinner with their grandparents. Don't you want that for your children?"

"I don't have children. And I don't have grandparents. Thanks for rubbing it in."

"Maybe you would if humans didn't destroy everything in our path."

"I don't have grandparents because humans are destroying the Earth? Now who's exaggerating?"

"The temperature of the Earth is rising steadily, there's so much trash in the ocean that people are kickstarting documentaries about it, and you can't eat several varieties of large fish anymore because they are so full of toxins that they are dangerous to eat."

"It's all perspective, buddy."

"Global warming is all perspective?"

"Nah, nah, I'll give you global warming, and maybe the fish too, but look at this life. We're in our thirties, we have great jobs. We own our homes, I have a picket fence, by the way, and I have vacation time and the money to spend on it. Things are so good now that we can sit in this car, a *Tesla*, listening to the Eagles on glorious FLAC files, while driving through a beautiful redwood forest that we have *not* destroyed, despite all your cynicism, and shoot the shit and make jokes about cholera."

"I'm not making jokes about cholera."

"You should be. We eradicated that shit. Now take that cassette tape and throw it out the window because I'm not playing it."

4. Side B

Hello?

Hi, Carl. It's me.

Renee, hi! What's up? You sound terrible.

…

Renee?

It's my … my … Jim's gone.

No. No way. Your brother? Gone? What do you mean? He's the healthiest 40-and-a-half-year-old I know. Was. Is... was.

Was... oh, Carl. I can't believe it. I can't even face it. How can this have happened?

I don't understand. He was just down camping the Lost Coast, wasn't he?

Yeah. There... oh, fuck, there was an accident.

Bike?

No, that's what's unbelievable. He was walking.

Walking?

Yeah. He was on his way to pick up takeout.

He always loved takeout after a good ride.

Exactly. He ordered food. We know that. The Thai place had called his phone seven times.

Seven?! What the fuck?

You know what I mean.

Oh, Renee, I'm so sorry. He's, I can't believe it. Man, I loved that guy. Always singing that damn "Desperado."

Yeah. It was his tune. He was always humming it.

Humming!?! Are you kidding me? Belting it out is more like it.

Yeah, I guess that's true.

Completely true, probably still an understatement. Did you ever go to karaoke with him?

Umm, I'm not sure.

When we were roommates in college we always went to that place in the warehouse district. The Otter Bar or something similar.

Yeah, I remember the place.

And he would sing "Desperado." In the worst way! Sometimes twice in one night!

No!

Yes! Hands down, *be-worst* karaoke singer ever. The lady who ran karaoke remembered him. "Oh, here he comes! *The* Desperado!"

Oh, wow. I never lived it, but I can definitely imagine it.

I lived it—maybe too many times. Aw. Oh, Jimmy. Big Jimmy.

Big? That's not Jim. You sure you even know him, Carl? You must be twice his size!

Yeah, yeah, I know. But he was big at heart.

Yes... he was. He was a pretty decent big brother, all things considered.

He was a pretty good friend to me too. Hey, remember how he would always make mashed potatoes?

So much butter.

Sooo much butter. And sometimes weed butter.

I knew it! Ha!

Haha. Oh, man. I've missed you Renie.

I've missed you too.

. . .

. . .

When's… Can I… Can I come with you to the…

Yes, yeah. Please. I can't go alone.

Good. I'd like that. Ren?

Yeah?

Is that "Desperado" I hear in the background?

Ya.

Oh, Renee.

Yeah… I'm going to miss him so much, Carl.

…

Carl?

Me too. Definitely going to miss him too. He was a great guy. I'll pick you up Friday, ok? And take you.

Yeah, okay, thanks.

And Renee?

Yeah?

Throw that tape out the window.

M'kay.

You don't need to be listening to that alone.

'kay.

5. A figurative eagle can't catch a mouse.

"I hate! This tape! It's the worst tape I've ever heard!"

"Tape!? It's an album."

"Album schmalbum."

"What!? How could you possible love me and say that?"

"Love you! What does that even mean? You find an Eagles tape, a blasted Eagles tape, to be as important as our marriage, as our love?!"

"Oh, don't exaggerate!"

"*I* shouldn't exaggerate? *I* shouldn't exaggerate!?"

"You know what I meant by that. You took one of my joys and insulted it. It's a symbol of me—of our love. You-"

"The Eagles have never been and will never be a symbol of our love. Nor has any cassette tape, ever, in the history of the world."

"You are literally breaking my heart right now."

"I'm literally breaking your heart? Did you even go to college?"

"And in the history of the world?! You don't think it's possible that other people in the world find music to be romantic, even symbolic of love? I find that quite hard to believe. In fact, when I was *in college*, I took a course on music and there is quite an important correlation between culture and music."

"Fine! I hate the Eagles! That's the truth. I have never, ever liked them."

"Our marriage was built on the Eagles!"

"Was! *Was* being the pivotal word in that sentence. I'm going to take this Eagles tape-"

"No!"

"And throw it out the window."

"No! No! No! You bitch! I can't believe you did that!"

"It's over."

"Yeah! You're right. It's over. Now. I can't handle being with someone who doesn't share my interests. Maybe that Eagles tape doesn't symbolize our love, but I loved it, and you might not know it, but every time I heard, 'Best of my Love,' when I was working at the bookstore during college, stocking books, it always, always made me think of you."

"Best of our love? It's T plus 2 years and all the shitty cassette tapes have been thrown away. It's time to throw this one out too."

"We used to be-"

"We used to be a lot of things. I used to be different, and so did you. Times change. *Life* changes."

"So you admit it, you changed! You're saying you changed."

"Hell, yeah I did!"

"Well I don't think so. I think you're just, just…"

"Just what? Spit it out."

"Fuck you. Spit it out. Actually, no, no. Just stop. I don't want this. This is not the person I am, nor is this the vacation I want… …yes, people change. How could they not?"

"Your interests suck."

"I- I still can't believe you threw that tape out the window."

"Are you crying?"

"No…"

"Over a mixed tape?"

"No. And it's not a mixed tape either."

"Well, then what is it? If you're not crying over the damn tape, then what is it?"

"That just-that literally rips my heart out."

"Oh, yeah? I *literally* broke your heart five minutes ago, and now I have *literally* ripped it out. *Wow*, I am a bitch. Tell me, did I reach my hand inside your body and rip your heart from inside of you?! You're an idiot!"

"Fine, fine. But you're a jerk! You and your 100 percent better than thou."

"Hahah, it's 'better than *thee*.'"

"That was my favorite tape. You literally threw it out the window and let it smash to pieces on the ground. Therefore, you have literally smashed to pieces a symbol of me, and of what I believe symbolized the love that I felt for you."

"Fine. I used to like the Eagles, and I used to like you. I don't know how we got from there to here, but here we are. Literally at the moment of decision making."

"You have figuratively broken my heart."

6. The Hitchhiker ruined it all.

Driving to the Shakespeare festival in Ashland, they took a scenic route through the redwoods. It was a special weekend, as they were celebrating their anniversary. On the way, they passed a hitchhiker, two, in fact.

Two hitchhikers were walking together, both men, hand in hand, both clearly foreign, and David felt a lump in his throat. He had to tell her.

He wasn't straight.

*   *   *

"I knew it!" she screamed at truly the top of her lungs. "I knew it when you insisted on buying this God damned Eagles tape!"

"Eagles tape? Grace, please! How- why are the Eagles suddenly inherently gay!? That's ridiculous."

"And you know what?"

"What?" he asked quietly as she rolled down her window and threw the tape violently to the pavement. He was sure that he didn't want to know.

"I don't even like Shakespeare! Awful, awful stuff! Ugh!" She scoffed so thickly it made him think of phlegm. Thick, caustic phlegm. And then he thought of Shakespeare, and the Eagles, and knew he'd done right.

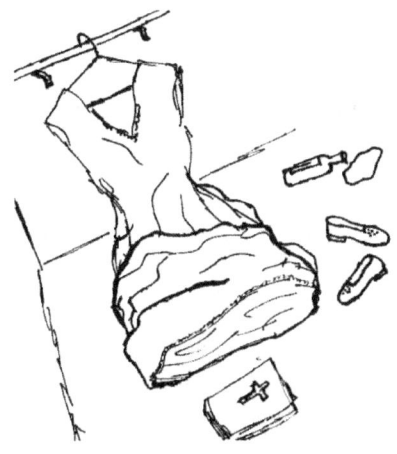

An Alternative Lifestyle

I picked up the phone to hear a mixture of sobs and gasps for air. This again. The wedding planning. If she thinks that I am on her side of this whole ordeal, then she has another thing coming. It was 9:18, and just enough free after-nine minutes had passed for another catastrophe to have occurred. I cannot imagine the current situation, as I usually cannot. It will be the most important day of her life, so I understand why she would be so concerned, but she is not usually the dramatic type, so it is a bit surprising that she has been so upset about all this. Lately, I would have to say that she has been making some bad choices. Weddings are a celebration of love, family, and tradition. Although maybe she has love, (or maybe not), she is certainly going in the opposite direction with both family and tradition. I do not know which wedding publications she has been reading, but I do not think that this is the time to make a point. Just why are her world views so important anyway?

I remember every moment of my wedding day. I took a whole summer off to plan, and I barely had enough time. I probably should have taken a lighter course load the previous semester, so that I could focus more on the details, but I am glad I kept going with my courses. I am just about to finish my sophomore year at the University, so I will be pregnant soon. I am ready to start my own family, and I am sure I will be giving birth to the first grandchild.

I was married last summer in my hometown Catholic Church with the local priest presiding and my grandparents sitting in the same pew that they do every Sunday. I married a man who converted to Catholicism for me—classes, white carnation and all—and I am now on the fast track to a medical profession and five kids. We already have a dog. My parents are more than content with my progress, and none too pleased with my sister's lifestyle choices. She has chosen to take a more *free-spirit* approach.

A grassy backyard wedding with casual, if not sloppy, dress and no priest was not what my family had in mind. My sister is quickly learning that planning a non-traditional wedding in a small town will not be a little girl's dream of building the perfect day. *Impossible* seems to be a better classification. The idea of a city wedding in the old Landmark Center was everything but flat-out rejected, and a destination wedding in Mexico was shot down with pleas of sudden withering grandparental health. The bombshell really dropped when my parents realized that to have a backyard wedding at six o'clock in the evening on a Saturday created a clear conflict with the family priest giving mass at the church at five-thirty. Why!? *Why* was the clear question; why would it be done any other way?

Last week's dilemma was the presence of alcohol at the blessed event. At my wedding, I was only 19, so this was not an issue. My husband and I drank sparkling white grape juice and a discreet cash bar was available for those who dared. My sister's fiancé has a hobby of beer tasting and even brewing his own, so he has been waiting for the day to have his favorites at his disposal. After much coaxing, the idea of alcohol being present was finally accepted, but the couple was forewarned of the many years that it took to build a reputation and how one drunken death could lead to its devastation. I do not know why they need alcohol anyway. If they find a good *deejay*, I am sure he will keep the dancing going well enough, and the smell of beer is just disgusting! Her dress will reek of it afterwards.

In mid-April, an unexpected strategy arose and my sister and her husband were legally married at a courthouse. I heard that it was because they were still being badgered about the lack of a priest for their ceremony. Well, legality *is* important, and suggestions of possible ministers and priests were still being offered regularly by family members and neighbors. I also heard that a couple of bridesmaids got together and contacted another local officiant, pretending to be the inquiring bride. This was a possibility for compromise, but I guess the bride and groom thought otherwise. Either way, they were now legally married, so the bickering had no option but to cease and the planning to continue. The extended family has, of course, taken part in the drama as well. I overheard my grandmother mention that since it was no longer a "real" wedding, she would be wearing slacks to the ceremony. Serves them right for rebelling, I guess.

About a month ago, there was a mutiny among the bridesmaids. The idea of unmatched black dresses was clearly a monstrosity to all. Some traditions must be kept. I was thinking the same thing, but I am only a personal attendant, so I kept my opinion to myself.

My sister was looking forward to the music for the ceremony the most. She loved all kinds of music, and had several friends and family members that she couldn't wait to hear sing and play. At one point she asked our very talented great aunt to accompany a nice religious piece. Finally, something to appease the grandparents! I guess she was blinded when she chose the piece, as she asked a Lutheran aunt to play a clearly Catholic hymn. Please. I believe things like this could have been avoided had she been a bit more thoughtful when working with others. She should have worked with her musicians to choose music that worked well for *everyone*. That is what I did, and it could not have gone more smoothly.

*   *   *

The culminating event is now rapidly approaching. I hope that she took my advice and hired a personal trainer to help her work out for the last few months. She is not overweight, but she should look her best. I read in one of my bridal magazines that 60 percent of women drop up to three dress sizes for their wedding day. I can see their reasoning. You will look back at the pictures for the rest of your life, so why not spend a little extra on getting rid of those love handles?

Oh! I just heard that she hired a *friend* to take the wedding pictures. I just cannot even imagine what she is thinking. Even if this friend graduated with a degree in photography, he still does not have *any* experience taking wedding photographs. Normally, a couple splurges on the photography. There were great packages at all the places we looked, most for under five thousand dollars. I got a great deal that even came with a painting of my husband and me, and it was completely worth it. Almost every room in our house has a picture of us on our wedding day. I even managed to make it the theme of one room. Beige walls and sheer curtains with a deep wine colored *valance* hanging over the curtain rod. There are several pictures hanging on the wall, as well as our painting, and a jar containing the dried petals that were thrown by the flower girls. On the corner table is our wedding album, and on one wall my dried wedding bouquet is hanging next to our marriage license. I love the room. It's where I always go when I just want to be alone.

*   *   *

Two days before the wedding, I traveled home to my parents' house. I rode with my eldest brother, who is a very good driver.

The night before the wedding, the grandparents called. Apparently, a great aunt and uncle were planning to give the couple a Bible as a wedding gift. Since they had already been legally married, they wanted to know the official marriage date to write in the Family History section of the Bible. I suppose they were right, it is the date they were legally married, but it wasn't truly necessary to call the night before the wedding. I guess this is what happens when you choose the non-conformist life. I cannot believe they cared, really; it is not like they were married in a real religious ceremony. I hope they straighten out their religious views before they have a family. That is no way to raise children. Where will they learn any morals?

The day of the wedding went as well as could be expected. There were a variety of things that were not as meticulously planned as they could have been. I doubt she had even given everyone a printed schedule of the day's events, as I had done. Well, they did cohabitate, so unfortunately; chances are she will have a second chance.

As the ceremony began, I did enjoy the Maria-chi music that began the processional. She even managed to find violin music for a cousin to play a very nice concerto. The timing was a little off; we could have probably run through the rehearsal a time or two more. I should really have just taken things over and done them right, but I will choose not to worry about that now. The violinist began, and my sister walked with both my parents down the grassy aisle under the canopy of trees. She looked rather pale in the white dress; I think a few times in the tanning bed would have been helpful. She *definitely* should have worn a necklace. We tried over and over again to convince her of that. I know she said that it made her uncomfortable, but it *is* her wedding day. You would think she could tough it out. That type of neckline should never go without some type of jewelry. My husband bought me an enchanting necklace with a diamond for my wedding day. I guess maybe they are not as financially stable as we were. I'm planning on being a surgeon, and my husband is studying management, so money really will not be an issue for us.

Standing at the front, they seemed quite happy together, but by the end of the first song, she had already requested a chair. I suppose she was rather drained from all the stress. She really was not very organized at all. I saw her wedding binder and it could have used some improvement. My parents were quite alarmed when she grabbed her matron of honor and rushed off the makeshift altar. Maybe she was having second thoughts.

Eventually, she made it back to the altar to finish the vows. She had merely been feeling ill and lightheaded. The vows were written by the couple, so it was quite nice, though I doubt she remembers much after the blacking out episode. Did I mention that her husband got his ring online? What a disgrace. Obviously he really *couldn't* care less. She may as well have woven flowers in her hair and played *Imagine*. At least he bought her a diamond. They probably should have just eloped like all the other hippies do.

Past Wishes

The woman's skin was well worn
And covered with wrinkles.
When she smiled, her face appeared
To be so well practiced in its lines,
That the expression was only natural.
Her eyes were filled with emotions of love
As she touched her granddaughter's cheek.
I saw the words form
As her wrinkles gracefully shifted
Around her smile pursed lips
And she spoke to her granddaughter.
...always be proud of who you are...
She smiled with acceptance
As she touched her grandmother's hand.
She was too young to fully understand
The wisdom of her grandmother's wrinkles,
But I saw, as she brought her arm
To rest on her lap, on her wrinkled skin
Below her wrist there were numbers,
And I understood her wrinkles.

Three Elizabeths Arrived

Three Elizabeths arrived. They all walked swiftly and confidently into the elevator of the Manhattan Municipal Building, the first in black round-toed pumps, the second in velvet chartreuse ballet flats, and the third in tall, silver-toed heels of pink that were far from the norm for nearly any given Elizabeth.

The first Elizabeth was wise—far too wise, in fact. Her life's work had been accomplished too soon and had left her pushing for more.

The second Elizabeth was a decade younger than the first. She was plain, but sweet; a good worker, but not the best. She had no problem living her life day after day after day. She had reasons for this. Satisfaction was bliss.

The third was quite the harlot. She had dyed black hair that held the type of big, rounded curls that reminded men of a pinup. She often found herself in situations like that, out of habit, no, but almost. She had a broken heart from so many years before. He had left her unjustly, the bastard. And she had shown him. She had danced and smiled and flirted and flung and been courted by so many men. So she had won. She'd read that he had been married in 1952; and she, in '51. He had been married twice. She was just getting rid of number 4. Unmistakably, she was more desirable.

The Elizabeths were not friends. It could even be said that they didn't know each other; but that's a lie. They did. When it came down to it, they were linked far, far too closely. The three Elizabeths all worked in the 40-story building at the intersection of Chambers and Centre Streets. The first Elizabeth was in research on one of the upper floors. Efficiently and with an unanticipated level of commitment and passion, she completed the types of fact checking and research which many a college student did each summer.

It is worth noting that it was the last Elizabeth, alone, that knew she was an Elizabeth in the company of two others. She was in payroll, and beyond her own perfectly intriguing escapades, she had a knack for watching, hearing, and therefore, monitoring, the many scandals of the tall grey tower.

She knew, for example, that each Monday afternoon, a certain courier boy and a certain lady of the upper management rendezvoused for lunch. She also knew that cash, and not necessarily a small amount of it, was exchanged in the 19th floor kitchen each month on the 19th day, whether a working day or not. Regarding Elizabeths, she also understood that the first Elizabeth was to be phased out soon, not because she wasn't a hard worker, but because technically, by certain, rather recent standards, she was unqualified. The degree she had, often laughed the third Elizabeth to herself, was nothing more than an MRS.

The middle Elizabeth, under the third Elizabeth's watchful eye, had fallen in love. She had subsequently fallen out of love. And back in. And out again, the poor thing. For such a normal looking Elizabeth, she had an uncanny ability to bump into single men on their very first day at the job. As a matter of fact, her current fellow fit the bill as well. The handsome, groomed, black suit of a man was the type of conqueror the third Elizabeth wouldn't have minded having as her fifth, if only she took seconds, which of course she did not. John James Waterman, as he was so aptly called, was new to the Beaux-Arts tower, though not new to the business, and had spent his last 27 years climbing towards the top of the pay scale. It just so happened that the second Elizabeth was in the break room the day he was being taken around. The third Elizabeth was aware of the fact that this was her strategy. She, the second Elizabeth, simply considered it good practice to be in the break room at opportune times such as these and those.

In the months since that first day near the decaf pot, the second Elizabeth had celebrated her morning break with him each Monday, Tuesday, Wednesday, and Friday. Thursday was for someone else.

Indeed, this is the moment that it could be mentioned that John James Waterman was not unmarried. He had been rather lumpily, if not unhappily, married for 24 years. Who else might be his wife, but the first Elizabeth? One can only assume they were not happy, as the only thing the first Elizabeth was interested in was her mind, her early marriage to John James Waterman no more than a stepping stone along the way. Just how very unfortunate it was that she was born in the year that she was and in the world that existed at that time. As is the situation versus any man, when she plateaued, he continued on up, not yet to this day having peaked. Poor Elizabeth.

The first Elizabeth wanted it all, and she unrightfully believed that she could have it. She worked hard, her house was beautiful, her husband handsome, and her children all invested in excellent schools.

Elizabeth the second had gone to the very same schools, all of the highest quality, that the three Waterman children attended. She knew it not, but she had. The first she had begun when she was young. There she had excelled until the moment that she'd become a woman. That was the day when her father had left. He had climbed to the top, the very top of his career ladder, that is. And then he had climbed further, to the ladder on the roof of a building he owned and ran, and proceeded to jump and send himself spiraling downward toward the gleaming revolving glass doors at the front of his very own building. Poor Elizabeth.

Her pleasant attendance at the first school soon ended. Her time at the second first-rate institution was impermanent. As a newfound woman, she did what she liked and she liked what she did. But alas, her term there ended as well. Her education at the third school was as short lived as the second. In truth, her diploma read the name of another school altogether, one that would cause the first Elizabeth to shudder at the very sound.

This last, particular remarkable happenstance was unbeknownst to the third Elizabeth, a surprising fact which she would have certainly relished knowing. However, as hard as a woman may try, an Elizabeth can never know everything, and implausible circumstances were just the thing that the third

Elizabeth very much wanted to envisage, but could not. Poor Elizabeth.

Three strong Elizabeths, each a knowing sparkle or a devious glint in their eye. How very unlikely that on the very day that all three Elizabeths arrived at the Municipal Building and filed into the elevator, there was no one else. Even more unbelievable was the fact that on that brisk morning, the elevator cable broke, plummeting not one, not two, but three Elizabeths to their quick and inevitable deaths, leaving the love of their lives alone; a man born as John James Waterman, but wanting wholly and entirely for his entire long and painful existence to be something and someone else entirely different. Poor Elizabeth.

Notes

[1] Past Wishes

"Past Wishes" was originally published on poetry.com.

[2] An Introduction to "The Screwtape Tales"

Several years back on an afternoon hike in Redwoods National Park, I found myself walking along the edge of Highway 199, the trail nowhere in sight.

As I followed the edge of the road, I came across some cassette tape film. It continued for forty, fifty feet, and more. Curious as I am, I was intrigued by the source of this tangled mess. I wondered what cassette tape it came from, and what small disaster caused its demise. Was it thrown angrily from a car window during a lovers' quarrel? Was this two-sided plastic case of overplayed tunes played on repeat from Tijuana to here until at last the solo driver tossed it out the window with the hope of never hearing it again? Was it a Garth Brooks tape? Harry Connick, Jr? Or much, much worse? Was it a high school mixed tape!?

And there it was, broken in two, yes. However, the title remained intact.

The Eagles.

The Eagles Greatest Hits.

I guess there are some things that can only be inspired by a love and/or hatred of the Eagles. "The Screwtape Tales" are a few of my best guesses. Following these musings, I can only admit that I am convinced that it must have been tragic, violent, serious, emotional, and clearly, desperate.

How meaningful it is that it was an Eagles tape, as only the Eagles it seems, could provoke all these intensely formidable emotions all in one swift throw from a car window. Whoever you are, my thoughts go out to you.

By the way, during the second story, entitled, *"Take it to the Limit," by the Eagles* I suggest playing the Eagles song of the same name as you read. The timing should work, but getting copyright permission didn't.

Good luck.

A good short story haunts you for life.

Patricia Willers is from rural Minnesota. By way of Guadalajara, Mexico and Leiden, The Netherlands, she currently resides in Davis, California, where she is a teacher. Her first novel, *Wandering Canalside*, was published in 2013.

Natalie Willers lives in rural Minnesota. She is currently a nursing student, adding to her existing background in science and Spanish. She is an avid reader of all genres and could easily qualify as owning her own library. Her love of reading was founded by her mother, enhanced by great authors, and is maintained by supporting Patricia's literary pursuits and always having a good book nearby. Furthermore, it is important to note that one should never challenge her in a Harry Potter trivia challenge.